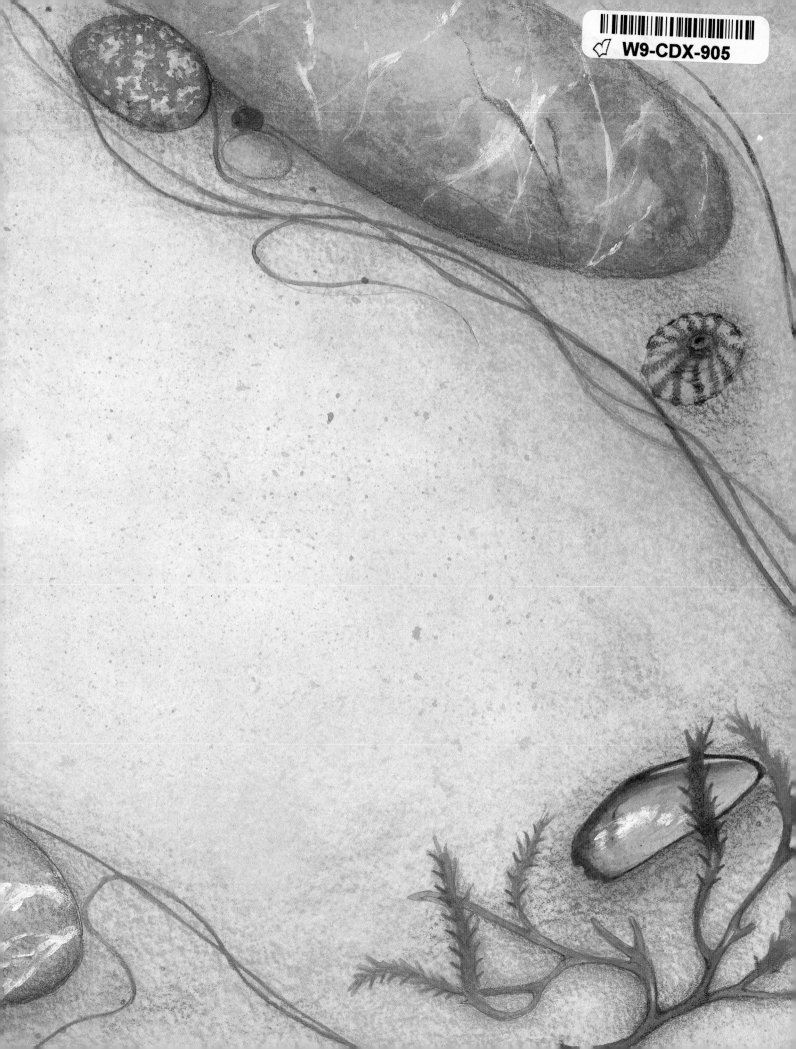

UP

BY Jim LaMarche

chronicle books · san francisco

"Hey, Mouse, have fun making cookies with Mommy today!" Michael yelled over the screeching gulls. "Dad and I will take care of the fishing."

"Cut it out, Michael," said Dad. "You'll get your turn, Mouse," he called back to Daniel. "When you're bigger." Then the *Toni Marie* turned toward the sea.

"I'm big enough now," Daniel grumbled from the pier steps. Other boys his age were already working on their dads' boats, helping with the nets, unloading the catch. He kicked a stone down the steps.

"Come on, Danny," said his mother. "Help me get started on the chowder."

"I'm tired of being little," said Daniel. "Someday I'll be stronger than Michael, and he won't tease me anymore."

"Probably," said his mom. "In the meantime, come help me peel these potatoes."

There was chowder for lunch, with handfuls of little oyster crackers. Daniel dropped some into his bowl. Mouse! They'd been calling him that since he was born. He hadn't used to mind it, even liked it once, but now he hated it. He poked at some crackers on the table. "Someday I'll be so strong," he mumbled. "I'll show Michael. . . ."

And then it happened. Something so strange, Daniel wasn't sure he could believe his eyes. One little cracker trembled for a second, then lifted up off the table. Not much. Not even an inch. Then, just as suddenly, it dropped right back down.

Daniel blinked. Had that really happened? *How*? Had *he* done it?

At the sink, Mom hadn't noticed a thing.

All afternoon and all the next day and all the *next* day, Daniel tried to make something—*anything*—move. He tried the oyster crackers again. Nothing. He tried buttons. He tried pins. He tried tiny feathers from a sofa pillow. For three days he'd been trying, but he hadn't been able to make it happen again. Nothing budged. Maybe he'd just imagined that the oyster cracker had lifted. Maybe it had never happened.

That night in the tub he felt worn out. Had the cracker lifted or hadn't it? Was he going crazy or what? Daniel picked up his old toy boat. He held it in the palm of his hand, closed his eyes, and imagined it was rising . . . rising . . . rising . . .

Suddenly Daniel couldn't feel the boat in his hand. His eyes snapped open. The boat was floating in the air! Not by much. Hardly an inch. But it *was floating!*

Michael banged on the door. "Hurry up, Mouse!" he yelled.

The little boat fell back down.

After that, whenever he was alone, Daniel practiced. He started by lifting little things—buttons and small seashells and pencil stubs. Then he tried forks and spoons, a hairbrush, and an old tin can behind the house. Every day, like a weightlifter, he got a little bit stronger. But though he could lift heavier things, he could never lift them high. Nor could he move them left or right. Never back and forth, just up, and that, not much.

One morning Daniel folded a paper airplane and gently thought it up. "Go! Fly!" he pleaded. But it didn't move. It just hung there, suspended in the air, until he stopped concentrating and it fell back down.

One afternoon Dad and Michael were unloading the catch off the boat. "I can help Dad," said Daniel, knowing he could. "I'm getting stronger," he added, knowing he was.

"You'll just spill the fish and make a mess of it," said Michael. "Go on home, Squeaky Mouse."

Dad shook his head. "Thanks, Mouse," he said. "But we're almost done here. Why don't you go clean your room? Make your mom happy."

Mouse, Mouse, Mouse. It was bad enough when *Michael* called him Mouse. Did *Dad* still have to do it, too?

Well, at least sweeping under his desk was easy now—he just lifted it up an inch or two. And he never spilled even a drop of fish water when he dusted.

"Nice job," said Mom. "You even got the dust bunnies from under your bed."

One Sunday afternoon, Dad stretched out on the sofa with the paper and was soon snoring. Daniel tiptoed in and hid behind the sofa.

Just for a warm-up, he lifted Dad's coffee cup and saucer. The spoon slipped off the saucer and clattered to the floor. Dad snorted, but was soon snoring again.

Daniel stared intently at his father. Gently, he began to lift him up.

Just then the kitchen door slammed. Mom and Michael. Daniel jumped. Dad plopped back down on the sofa.

"What? What?!" he sputtered. "Mouse, is that you?"

Daniel held his breath and didn't move. Finally Dad put his head back down and went back to sleep.

When Mom and Michael came in, Daniel was lying on the floor reading the comics. "Shhhhh. Dad's sleeping," he whispered.

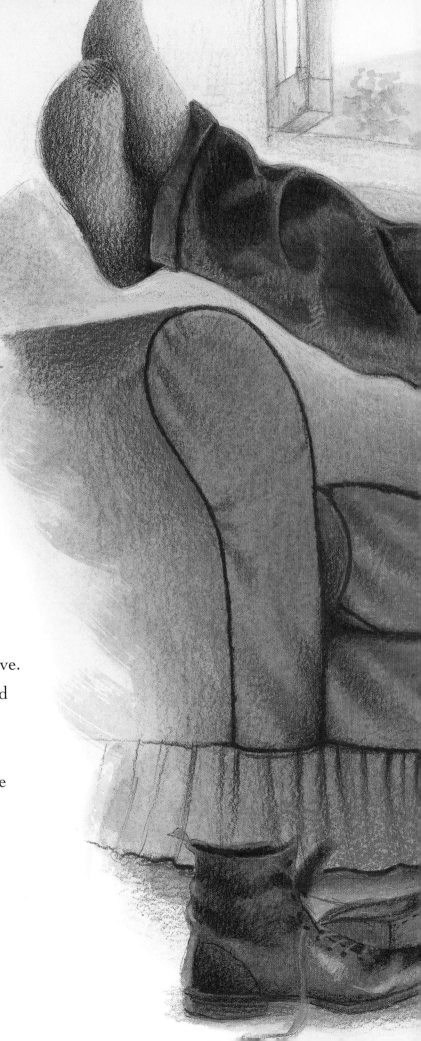

As the days passed, Daniel's ability got stronger and stronger. He could lift bigger and bigger things. But it was always the same. Never left or right. Never back and forth. Just up. And that, not much. What was the use of this? he wondered.

Then one evening when he was coming in for dinner, Mom asked, "Did you see Dad and Michael at the dock?" Daniel hadn't. "Maybe we'd better go see what's taking them so long," she said.

The *Toni Marie* was
in, tied up to the dock,
but Michael and Dad
weren't around. Daniel and
his mother started walking
along the cliffs. They heard the
shouts before they got to the cove.

"Look, Daniel!" cried Mom.
"That poor whale has beached itself."

"Will it die?" Daniel asked.

"If it can't get back to deep water, yes,"
said Mom.

Dad, Michael, and the other fishermen
were pulling and pushing with all their strength,
but the whale wasn't moving.

"Come on, Mom!" Daniel shouted. "We've got to help."

The men looked worried. "We've been here for an hour," said Dad, "and we haven't been able to budge this poor whale even an inch."

"I think I can help," said Daniel softly.

Michael laughed out loud. A few of the men smiled. But Daniel's father didn't laugh. He looked at Daniel strangely, as if he were studying him.

"I think Mouse is a lot stronger than he looks, Michael," he said. "Let's all try it one more time."

The men returned to their places around the whale. His mother took off her shoes and socks and joined them. Daniel moved to the whale's side. He placed his hands on the smooth skin. He looked into the whale's eye. Then he shut his eyes and concentrated.

Daniel heard the water lapping softly against his legs. He heard the gulls screeching overhead and the seals sniffing further out in the water. He thought he heard the whale sigh. He felt the whale's cool skin and his fingers tingled. His heart pounded. He seemed to feel the whale's blood in his own veins. And then he felt calm.

Slowly, slowly, so slowly no one even noticed it, the whale lifted up. Not much. But with everyone pushing, not much was enough. The whale edged slowly back into deeper water. Further and further, until finally it was deep enough to swim.

Then, with a couple of strokes of its huge tail, the whale turned and swam away, free.

Everyone splashed one another and danced on the beach and cheered.
No one knew how they had ever been able to do it, but wasn't it wonderful that
they had, they marveled. Laughing and clapping one another on the back, they
all went home to supper.

But Daniel and Michael and their parents stood there a while longer.
Finally Daniel's father spoke.

"We'd better get going," he said. "We could use some supper, too. And you need to get to bed early tonight, Daniel." He smiled. "The *Toni Marie* leaves at dawn."

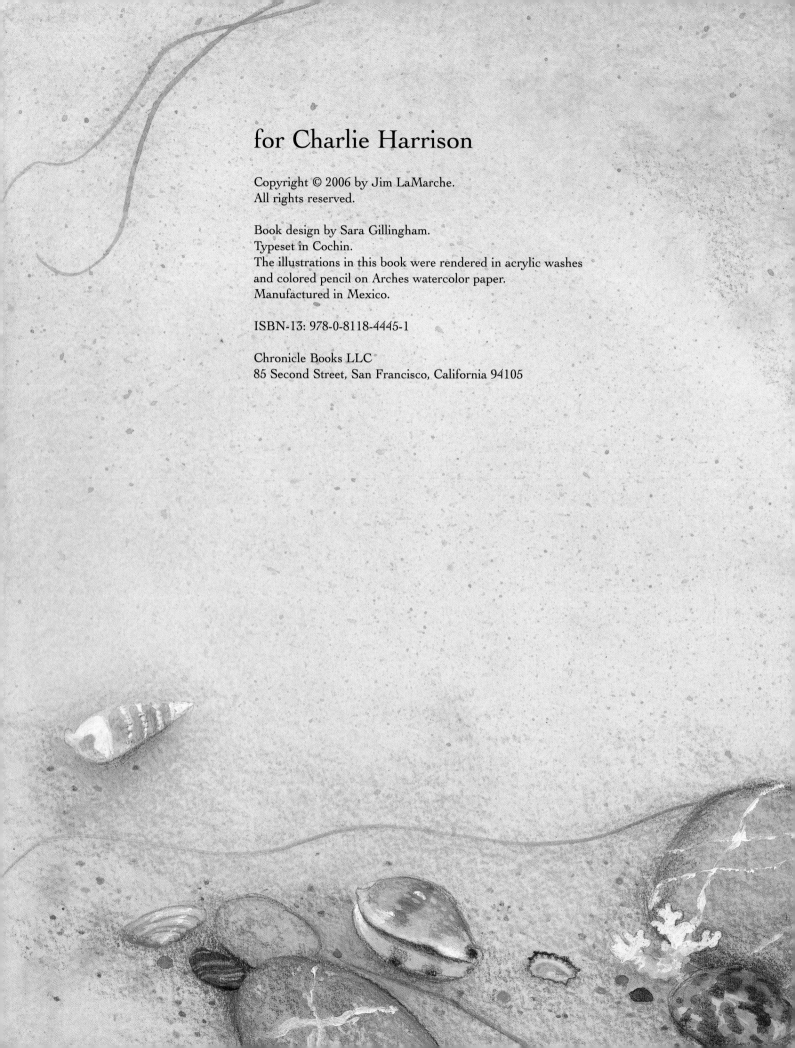

for Charlie Harrison

Book design by Sara Gillingham.
Typeset in Cochin.
The illustrations in this book were rendered in acrylic washes
and colored pencil on Arches watercolor paper.
Manufactured in Mexico.

ISBN-13: 978-0-8118-4445-1

Chronicle Books LLC
85 Second Street, San Francisco, California 94105